Karen's Island Adventure

Look for these and other books about Karen in the Baby-sitters Little Sister series:

1 *Karen's Witch*
2 *Karen's Roller Skates*
3 *Karen's Worst Day*
4 *Karen's Kittycat Club*
5 *Karen's School Picture*
6 *Karen's Little Sister*
7 *Karen's Birthday*
8 *Karen's Haircut*
9 *Karen's Sleepover*
#10 *Karen's Grandmothers*
#11 *Karen's Prize*
#12 *Karen's Ghost*
#13 *Karen's Surprise*
#14 *Karen's New Year*
#15 *Karen's in Love*
#16 *Karen's Goldfish*
#17 *Karen's Brothers*
#18 *Karen's Home Run*
#19 *Karen's Good-bye*
#20 *Karen's Carnival*
#21 *Karen's New Teacher*
#22 *Karen's Little Witch*
#23 *Karen's Doll*
#24 *Karen's School Trip*
#25 *Karen's Pen Pal*
#26 *Karen's Ducklings*
#27 *Karen's Big Joke*
#28 *Karen's Tea Party*
#29 *Karen's Cartwheel*
#30 *Karen's Kittens*
#31 *Karen's Bully*
#32 *Karen's Pumpkin Patch*
#33 *Karen's Secret*
#34 *Karen's Snow Day*
#35 *Karen's Doll Hospital*
#36 *Karen's New Friend*
#37 *Karen's Tuba*
#38 *Karen's Big Lie*
#39 *Karen's Wedding*
#40 *Karen's Newspaper*
#41 *Karen's School*
#42 *Karen's Pizza Party*
#43 *Karen's Toothache*
#44 *Karen's Big Weekend*
#45 *Karen's Twin*
#46 *Karen's Baby-sitter*
#47 *Karen's Kite*
#48 *Karen's Two Families*
#49 *Karen's Stepmother*
#50 *Karen's Lucky Penny*
#51 *Karen's Big Top*
#52 *Karen's Mermaid*
#53 *Karen's School Bus*
#54 *Karen's Candy*
#55 *Karen's Magician*
#56 *Karen's Ice Skates*
#57 *Karen's School Mystery*
#58 *Karen's Ski Trip*
#59 *Karen's Leprechaun*
#60 *Karen's Pony*
#61 *Karen's Tattletale*
#62 *Karen's New Bike*
#63 *Karen's Movie*
#64 *Karen's Lemonade Stand*
#65 *Karen's Toys*
#66 *Karen's Monsters*
#67 *Karen's Turkey Day*
#68 *Karen's Angel*
#69 *Karen's Big Sister*
#70 *Karen's Grandad*
#71 *Karen's Island Adventure*
#72 *Karen's New Puppy*

Super Specials:
1 *Karen's Wish*
2 *Karen's Plane Trip*
3 *Karen's Mystery*
4 *Karen, Hannie, and Nancy: The Three Musketeers*
5 *Karen's Baby*
6 *Karen's Campout*

Little Sister

Karen's Island Adventure

Ann M. Martin

Illustrations by Susan Tang

A
LITTLE APPLE
PAPERBACK

SCHOLASTIC INC.
New York Toronto London Auckland Sydney

The author gratefully acknowledges
Stephanie Calmenson
for her help
with this book.

ISBN 0-590-26194-0

12 11 10 9 8 7 6 5 4 3 2 1 6 7 8 9/9 0 1/0

Printed in the U.S.A. 40

First Scholastic printing, March 1996

New Month, New House

"Karen, breakfast is almost ready!" called Mommy.

"I will be downstairs in a minute," I replied.

I jumped out of bed and got dressed. I wanted to wear an extra nice outfit in honor of moving day. You see, it was the first day of March. That meant I was moving from my little house to my big house. (I will tell you later why I have two houses.) I put on a light blue shirt with my green and blue striped tights. Then I put on my green corduroy jumper.

I looked in the mirror.

"Perfectamento," I said to myself.

In case you are wondering, my name is Karen Brewer. I am seven years old. I have blonde hair, blue eyes, and a bunch of freckles. I have two pairs of glasses. I wear the blue pair for reading. I wear the pink pair the rest of the time.

There was one more thing I wanted to do before breakfast. I wanted to say good-bye to my little-house dolls and pets. I said a special good-bye to Goosie, my stuffed cat.

"Thank you for being a very good February friend," I told him.

I had needed all the friends I could get in February. It had been a hard month. First of all, my grandad died. I loved him and miss him very much. He and Granny had been living with us since before Thanksgiving. After Grandad died, Granny moved back home to her farm in Nebraska. I talk to her on the phone all the time. But I still miss having her around.

So I was glad it was a new month. I was glad I was going to a new house. And I was glad it was going to be a new season soon. At the end of March, it would be spring.

At the beginning of March, my school will have a spring break. Guess what I am doing with my big-house family. Just in case you cannot guess, I will tell you.

We are spending the week at Palm Isle, a resort on the island of St. Philip in the Caribbean. I am gigundoly excited about the trip.

"I wish I could take you with me, Goosie," I said. "You could use a vacation. But if I take you along, I have to take everyone. And there is not enough room in my suitcase for everyone."

Goosie did not look like he minded too much. He is a homebody at heart.

"Karen? Are you coming?" called Mommy.

Oops. It was getting late. My good-byes were taking longer than I thought. I ran downstairs to the kitchen.

"I am here!" I said. "Good morning, Mommy! Good morning, Seth! Good morning, Andrew!"

Andrew is my little brother. He is four going on five. Seth is my stepfather. I do not know exactly how old he is.

I sat down at my place. A bowl of Krispy Krunchy cereal with sliced bananas was waiting for me.

"Do you have all your things packed for your move to the big house?" asked Seth.

"I think so," I replied.

I do not need to carry too many things back and forth. That is because I am a two-two. Wait. You do not know what a two-two is. I guess I have some explaining to do.

Being a Two-Two

A long time ago when I was little, I lived in one house in Stoneybrook, Connecticut, with Mommy, Daddy, and Andrew. Then Mommy and Daddy started fighting a lot. They tried to work things out. But they just could not do it. They told Andrew and me that they love us very much. But they did not love each other enough to live together anymore. So they got divorced.

Mommy moved with Andrew and me to a little house not too far away from the big house. Then she met Seth. Mommy and

Seth got married. That is how Seth became my stepfather. So here is who lives at the little house: Mommy, Seth, Andrew, me, Midgie (Seth's dog), Rocky (Seth's cat), Emily Junior (my pet rat), and Bob (Andrew's hermit crab).

The house I am going to after school is the big house. Daddy stayed there after the divorce. (It is the house he grew up in.) After the divorce Daddy met someone new, too. Her name is Elizabeth. She and Daddy got married. So now Elizabeth is my stepmother. Elizabeth was married once before and has four children. They live at the big house also. They are David Michael, who is my age; Kristy, who is thirteen and the best stepsister ever; and Sam and Charlie, who are so old they are in high school.

Two more people live at the big house. One of them is my sister, Emily Michelle. She is two and a half. She was adopted from a faraway country called Vietnam. I love her a lot. That is why I named my pet rat after her.

The other person I did not tell you about yet is Nannie. She is Elizabeth's mother. That makes her my stepgrandmother. She came to live at the big house so she could help take care of Emily. But really she helps take care of everyone.

Do you want to know about the pets who live at the big house? I will tell you. They are Shannon, David Michael's big Bernese mountain dog puppy; Boo-Boo, Daddy's cranky old cat; Crystal Light the Second, my goldfish; and Goldfishie, Andrew's alligator (just kidding!). Emily Junior and Bob usually come to live at the big house with Andrew and me. But we left them at the little house this time because of our trip.

Now I will tell you about being a two-two. Andrew Two-Two and Karen Two-Two are the special names I gave to my brother and me. (I got those names from a book my teacher read in class. It is called *Jacob Two-Two Meets the Hooded Fang*.) The reason we are two-twos is because we have two of so many different things. We have two houses and two families, two mommies and two daddies, two cats and two dogs. We each have two sets of clothes, toys, and books. I have two bicycles, one at each house. Andrew has two tricycles. I have two stuffed cats. Moosie lives at the big house. And you know that Goosie lives at the little house. I have two pieces of Tickly, my special blanket. Having two of lots of things makes it easier to go back and forth because we do not have to pack as much.

I also have two best friends. Nancy Dawes lives next door to the little house. Hannie Papadakis lives across the street and one house over from the big house. We call ourselves the Three Musketeers because we like to do everything together. Well, almost everything.

Hannie and Nancy are not coming to St. Philip with me, of course. That is too bad. Because I know one thing for sure. My island vacation is going to be a sensation!

Getting Ready

It was Friday afternoon. I hopped off the school bus and raced down the street. I was on my way to the big house.

Daddy was outside waiting for me. He scooped me up in his arms.

"I am happy you are here!" he said.

"Me, too," I replied.

Andrew was already home. He was in the kitchen having a snack with Emily.

"Karen!" said Emily. She reached up sticky jelly hands. I let her hug me because I love her.

I waved hi to Andrew. He waved back with jelly fingers and a mouth full of crackers.

Then I got a big hug from Nannie. "Come join us," she said.

I was on my fourth cracker with cream cheese and jelly when Kristy came home from school.

"Hi, Karen. Hi, Andrew," said Kristy. She bent over to give us hugs. But she jumped back as soon as she saw our jelly fingers.

Sam and Charlie walked in next. They looked at our grape jelly mustaches and started to laugh.

"Hi, funny faces," said Sam.

By the time Elizabeth returned from work, we were all cleaned up. She thought she had the cleanest kids in Stoneybrook. (Ha!)

At dinner Daddy said, "Our vacation countdown begins tonight. A week from tomorrow we will be on our way."

We talked about all the exciting things

we were going to do. When we finished dinner, we went into the living room and looked at brochures. They told about Palm Isle. We had seen them all before. But with seven days to go everything looked more exciting.

"It says the Palm Isle Resort boasts the most activities of any resort of its kind," read Elizabeth.

There sure were a lot of activities. There was boating, waterskiing, windsurfing, golfing, snorkeling, volleyball, and tennis. There were movies, singalongs, and shows. There was a library, a game room, and a mini shopping center. There were pages and pages filled with things to do.

"I want to do some of this," said Daddy.

He pointed to a man lying in a hammock under a shady tree reading a book.

Just then I remembered something important. Elizabeth had reminded us that Daddy's birthday fell on the last day of our vacation. I wanted to buy him a gigundoly good present while we were there.

ISLAND
FUN
Caribbean
Vacation
ST. PHILIP

I also wanted to buy souvenirs for my friends and me.

"Excuse me," I said. "I am going upstairs now. Good night, everyone."

As soon as I reached my room I counted my savings. Not bad. But it could be better. I would have to save my allowance during the week. And maybe I could do a couple of jobs. I knew Nannie would pay me to dust her room. And maybe Elizabeth would pay me to watch Emily.

The week went by in a blur. I packed a little bit every day. And I saved a little more money for my trip.

By Thursday, I had three dollars and fifty cents more than when I started. And when I hopped off the school bus on Friday, I found a quarter on the street!

"Have a great trip," said Hannie.

"Thanks. I will see you in ten days!" I replied.

I raced to the big house. I was finally on vacation. In the morning I would be going with my family to St. Philip.

Up, Up, and Away!

It was still dark outside when we woke up on Saturday morning. We were catching a very early flight to Miami.

We had finished packing the night before. All that was left to do was get dressed, eat breakfast, and drive to the airport.

At five-thirty in the morning these things are not so easy. First I put my shirt on backwards. Then I could not find one of my socks. Next I spilled orange juice on my lap and had to change my pants.

But by six-fifteen I was in the van and buckling up with everyone else. As soon as we were on the road, I sang a song to get us into the island spirit. It was a song from Trinidad we sang at school about a very busy donkey.

"My donkey walk. My donkey talk. My donkey eat with a knife and fork. Tingalayo! Come, little donkey, come! Tingalayo! Come, little donkey, come!"

Next we all sang "A Hundred Coconuts on a Tree." This is how we sang it: *"A hundred coconuts on a tree. A hundred on a tree. If one of those coconuts fell on me, ninety-nine coconuts on a tree!"*

We were down to the last few coconuts when Daddy pointed out the first airport signs.

"Remember, we will be taking three different planes today," said Elizabeth. "The first one goes to Miami, Florida. The second goes to the Bahamas."

"Ooh! Can we stop and visit?" I asked.

Everyone except Nannie and Emily had been to the Bahamas before. That trip was really fun.

"We will not have time," said Daddy. "The third plane will be waiting to take us to St. Philip."

Daddy parked the car in the airport lot. Then we piled our bags into carts and wheeled them inside to the baggage check-in counter.

I have been on airplanes a few times already. So I know all about airports and checking in.

But this was Emily's first airplane trip. She started crying at the baggage counter. She did not want anyone taking our bags away.

"You do not have to worry," I said. "Our bags do not want to sit with us anyway. They will be much happier traveling with the other bags going to St. Philip. They will meet us there."

Emily stopped crying and waved goodbye to the bags.

"Thank you," Elizabeth whispered to me.

Then came the announcement for our plane.

"Flight One-oh-one to Miami, Florida, now boarding at Gate Sixteen."

"Let's go," said Daddy.

We walked to our gate. A big crowd of people was waiting there. As soon as the ten of us arrived, the crowd was even bigger.

"We sure picked a popular flight," said Kristy.

It took awhile for everyone to board the plane and find their seats. My family took up one whole row. In each row were three seats, an aisle, four seats, another aisle, then three more seats. Here is how we sat: In the first group, David Michael, Sam, and Charlie. In the center group, Daddy, Elizabeth, Emily, and Nannie. In the last group, Kristy, Andrew, and me. (I got to sit next to the window.)

We listened to the flight attendant make

a speech about safety. Then we all held hands straight across the row. The plane rolled down the runway and started to rise. Soon we were up, up, and away!

The first plane was big. It flew to Miami. The second plane was smaller. It flew to the Bahamas. The third plane was tiny. The ride was noisy, bumpy, and fun! By the time we touched the ground in St. Philip, I was so excited I could hardly keep still.

"Hello, St. Philip!" I cried. "I am gigundoly happy to see you!"

Welcome to Palm Isle

The first thing I noticed when we stepped off the plane was the temperature. It was *hot*. And the sun. It was *bright*.

I dug into my knapsack and pulled out my new sunglasses. They had yellow frames with white speckles. When I put them on I felt like a glamorous movie star on a tropical vacation. I held my arms out wide and lifted my chin in the air.

"Halloo, dahlings," I said. "Which way to Palm Isle?"

Beep! Beep! A van with "Palm Isle Resort"

written on the side was waiting at the curb. The van was turquoise with brightly colored fruits painted on the side.

The driver had very dark skin and a big friendly smile. He welcomed his passengers to St. Philip.

"You must be the famous movie star from the States," he said when I got on the bus.

I laughed and peeked at him from under my glasses.

"I'm really just Karen Brewer," I replied. "But maybe some day I will be famous."

"Welcome to the island, Karen," said the driver. "My name is Robert. Just sit back and enjoy the ride."

I hoped Robert was going to talk some more. His words sounded very pretty, almost as if he were singing.

The ride in the van was even bumpier than the plane. I looked out the window. The road was very narrow. I kept thinking we were going to hit a car or a biker. But somehow there was enough room for everyone.

Around us was lots of tall green grass. Then I saw a glimmer of blue up ahead.

"Everyone, look!" I said.

I pointed to the water. It was the prettiest blue I had ever seen.

"That is the Caribbean Sea," Robert said. "On the other side of the island is the Atlantic Ocean. The Caribbean is nice and smooth. No waves."

"You can go swimming later if you want," said Daddy.

We passed by trees with bright birds and fruits.

"Look at those houses," said Kristy. "There are no houses like that in Stoneybrook."

They looked like gingerbread houses. They were yellow, pink, green, and blue. In almost all the windows white curtains were blowing in the breeze.

Emily waved to a little girl sitting on the steps of her house with her mommy. The girl waved back.

I liked St. Philip. It was a friendly island.

Beep! Beep!

"We are here," said the driver. "Welcome to Palm Isle."

We drove onto the hotel grounds. The resort looked like nothing on the rest of the island. The grass was neat and trim. I could see the golf course, the tennis courts, two pools, lots of beach chairs and umbrellas, and a snack bar.

I thanked Robert for the excellent ride. Then we went into the air-conditioned lobby to check in.

Daddy got the keys to our rooms. The ten of us filled two elevators. It took three porters to wheel our bags upstairs.

I was sharing a room with Kristy and Emily. It was pink and white and beautiful. We could see the water from our window.

I dropped my knapsack on the floor and threw myself onto one of the beds. I felt like the luckiest kid in the world.

Signing Up

When we finished unpacking, my big family and I piled back into two elevators and went to the hospitality desk.

"Welcome to Palm Isle," said the man at the desk. "I am Ron, your hospitality director. I would like you to meet Laura, your host for the week. She will show you around and answer any questions you may have."

Laura smiled at us. "Hello, everyone!" she said. "My, this is a big family. I just love big families."

Laura was very bubbly. She looked a little older than Sam and Charlie, but not as old as Daddy and Elizabeth.

"Hi, Laura," I said. "I'm Karen."

"Hi, Karen," replied Laura. "I will do my best to remember all your names. But if I forget, you will have to help me out."

"Do not worry," I said. "I will help you."

One by one the people in my family introduced themselves. Then Laura took us on a tour of the grounds. While we were walking around she told us about Palm Isle.

"We have two clubs for children," said Laura. "Two- to four-year-olds can spend weekday mornings at the Dolphin Club. Five- to twelve-year-olds can join the Island Club. For anyone over twelve we have all kinds of lessons, activities, tournaments, and water sports."

"I want to be in the Island Club," I said.

"Me, too," said David Michael.

"Come, we will get you signed up," said Daddy.

"I will take Andrew and Emily to join the

Dolphin Club," said Elizabeth.

"I am going right over to sign up for the golf tournament," said Nannie.

We all stopped and looked at Nannie.

"Golf?" said Charlie. "You play golf?"

We know Nannie is an excellent bowler. She has even won trophies. We did not know she was a golfer, too.

"Oh, I've golfed a bit in my day," replied Nannie. "Anyway, the tournament is open to anyone thirteen and over. It is being held on Friday. I will sign up for lessons and games during the week. By Friday I will be ready to win."

"I am sure you will be a very good golfer," said Laura. "But remember there may be people here who golf all the time. It might be hard to beat them."

"I will just work harder than they do," replied Nannie. She returned to the activities desk to sign up.

Charlie and Kristy signed up for windsurfing. Sam was still deciding what to do.

Elizabeth took Andrew and Emily to join the Dolphin Club. And Daddy took David Michael and me to join the Island Club. A girl was on line in front of us with her parents. She looked just my age.

"I am not sure I want to join a club," I heard her say.

"But you can swim and play games with other children," said her mother.

"The activity will be good for you," said her father.

The girl seemed worried. But she signed up anyway. Then she followed her parents while they picked out the things they wanted to do. They had a long list.

After my family had signed up for their activities, we all put on bathing suits and went for a swim in the ocean. (Really Emily went for a splash. She does not know how to swim yet.)

Then we returned to our rooms to dry off and get ready for dinner. There were three restaurants at Palm Isle. We decided to try

Coconut Creek first. When we arrived, we were given their biggest table. It was right by a window.

"Can we explore the island tomorrow?" I asked.

"That is a good idea," replied Daddy. "We will do that first thing in the morning."

All right! I could hardly wait.

A Surprise Tour

We ate an early breakfast on Sunday. Then we went to the hospitality desk. We found out that a hotel bus was giving a tour of the island.

"I think it would be more fun to go on our own," said Daddy. "I have an idea. I will be right back."

Daddy found Robert, our bus driver. He knew someone who could help us.

"My cousin, Trevor, is a taxi driver. He knows all the best places to go," said Robert.

Ten minutes later we were piling into Trevor's van. Trevor was just as nice as Robert. I could tell our tour was going to be fun.

"Is there anything special you would like to see on the island?" asked Trevor. "Or should I surprise you?"

"I love surprises!" I said.

"We will leave our tour to you," said Daddy.

"Let me see," said Trevor. "Ah, yes. I know just the place. It is on the other side of the island."

Along the way Trevor pointed out lots of churches. And he showed us the school his children go to. It was a long wooden building with a porch around it. It did not look anything like Stoneybrook Academy.

"Over there are sugar plantations. We grow a lot of sugar on St. Philip. That is why our island is so sweet," said Trevor with a smile.

We drove up a steep hill and down the other side.

"Wow! Look at the water," said David Michael.

"That must be the Atlantic Ocean," said Sam.

"Is that our surprise?" I asked.

"No, it is not," replied Trevor. "Wait and see."

We drove along the coast to the tip of the island. A wood sign stuck in sandy ground said *Pekita's Cave*.

"Who is Pekita?" asked Kristy.

"You will meet her soon," replied Trevor.

Daddy paid for us to go inside and we drove through the gate.

"Maa! Maa!" A black and white sheep trotted to the van to say hello.

"Here is Pekita," said Trevor. "Later she will join us for lunch. You better watch out. She loves orange soda."

I waved good-bye to Pekita as we walked into the cave.

"See you later," I said.

We were the only ones inside. We walked

a little way and soon we saw huge columns of stone. They seemed to be growing from the roof and the walls. Some seemed to be growing up from the ground.

"The stones hanging down are called stalactites. The stones growing up are called stalagmites," said Trevor. "It took thousands of years for them to grow."

The cave was becoming darker and darker. Emily started whining. I think she was scared. Then we turned a corner and saw the sun. And we could see the ocean!

There were openings in the rock walls, like windows. The windows were in the shape of animals. I peered through a whale window. The ocean splashed my face. It was fun being inside and out at the same time.

"This place is cool," said David Michael, looking through a pony-shaped window.

I ran to one shaped like a cat's head.

"This was an excellent surprise," I said to Trevor.

We zigzagged through the cave and came

out where we started.

"Lunchtime," said Trevor.

I bought a fish sandwich and a bottle of orange soda at the refreshment stand. I was almost finished eating when Pekita nuzzled me.

I tipped the bottle up so she could take a drink. She finished every drop of soda. Then she licked the bottle.

"Maa!" said Pekita.

"You are welcome," I replied.

The Island Club

I jumped out of bed Monday morning and got dressed fast. It was going to be my first day at the Island Club.

My family ate breakfast in the coffee shop. Then we went our separate ways. Elizabeth and Daddy took Emily and Andrew to the Dolphin Club. Then they were going to take a swim. Charlie and Kristy headed for the beach to go windsurfing. David Michael and I went to the poolhouse where the Island Club was meeting.

"Have fun, everyone," called Nannie.

She was on her way to her first golf class.

"I will walk with you," said Sam. "I decided to play golf, too."

Huh? I knew Sam had taken golf classes in high school. But I did not think he liked them. Oh, well. He would probably have more fun golfing on St. Philip.

When David Michael and I arrived at the poolhouse a bunch of kids had already gathered round. There were also two counselors. They looked about the same age as Sam and Charlie. They were wearing T-shirts that said *Island Club Staff* and sun visors with their names written on them. They were Jenny and Mark.

"Are you kids signed up for the club?" asked Jenny.

"Yup," I replied.

"Great. We are waiting for a few more kids to show up. I am your head counselor, Jenny. This is my assistant counselor, Mark," said Jenny.

The girl who had been on line ahead of me on Saturday was already at the poolhouse. I was glad she was there. The other kids looked either older or younger than me.

"Hi," I said to her. "My name is Karen. What's your name?"

"Sandy," replied the girl.

That was all she said. I asked how old she was.

"Seven," she replied. She did not ask how old I was. I told her anyway. Then I told her where I was from.

"I live in Stoneybrook, Connecticut. Where do you live?"

"Rhode Island."

She did not say any more. I guessed she was shy. I tried again to be friendly.

"I think this club will be fun, don't you?" I said.

"Uh-huh."

"Okay, kids. Here is the plan," said Jenny. "First, you are all going to get sun visors like mine. You can decorate them with your names. That way we can get to know each other. We have markers, squeeze paints, glitter, and glue. If you need anything else just holler."

Oh, goody. I like to holler. When I holler at home or in school, grown-ups remind me to use my indoor voice. Now I could holler anytime I wanted.

I picked up one of the sun visors and set to work. I squirted glue in the shape of the letter K on the front. Then I sprinkled hot pink glitter on it. I made every letter of my name a different color.

While the sun visors were drying, we went to the beach to swim. Jenny told us to pick water buddies.

"Do you want to be my buddy today?" I asked Sandy.

Sandy shook her head. "I am not going swimming." She walked away before I could ask why.

A girl named Sara picked me to be her buddy. Jenny started a game of freeze tag in the water. It was fun.

Then we went for a seashell hunt on the beach. Sandy seemed to like that. Sandy was quiet. So maybe she only liked to do quiet things.

I am noisy. But I like to do everything. Noisy things *and* quiet things.

I loved my first day at the Island Club. I would love it even better if Sandy would be my Island Club friend.

Shopping for Souvenirs

On Monday afternoon Kristy and I went shopping in town with a group of people from the hotel. I wanted to buy souvenirs for Mommy, Seth, Hannie, and Nancy. And I wanted to get something special for Daddy's birthday. Robert drove the van to town.

"How do you like it here so far?" he asked.

"I do not like it," I said. "I *love* it!"

"That is what I like to hear," replied Robert.

We reached the town in no time. It was bustling with people. The biggest crowd was at the Cheap-Stop Food Market. It took up about four blocks. Everywhere you looked were tables piled high with fruits and vegetables. The people behind the tables were wearing fruit-colored clothes — lime green, banana yellow, watermelon pink.

"Can we stop and get something here?" I asked Kristy. "The bus was hot and I am thirsty."

"Me, too," replied Kristy. "But we have to hurry. We want to leave enough time to shop for souvenirs."

We found a very cute little watermelon and decided to share it. When the woman who had sold it to us cut it open, we were surprised. It was yellow inside instead of pink.

"Taste it," she said. "It is sweet and juicy."

Kristy and I tasted the watermelon. It was the best we had ever eaten. We giggled at how much juice dribbled down our chins.

While we ate, we walked along a narrow, winding street. We stopped at a sign that said *Sally's Souvenir Shop*.

"I bet I can say that three times fast," I said. "Sally's Souvenir Shop. Sally's Souvinseer Sop. Sassy's Soupincheer Chop."

"Come, Karen. Let's go inside," said Kristy, laughing.

Everything in the store had "St. Philip" written on it. Those things would be good souvenirs. But they did not seem to be good birthday gifts for Daddy.

"Let me know if I can help with anything," said the woman behind the counter.

She was wearing a seashell necklace that I liked. A small St. Philip's coin was hanging from it.

"Are there any more necklaces like that?" I asked.

"Right over here," she replied.

She pointed to a necklace stand at the far end of the counter. I picked out the prettiest one for Mommy.

"Karen, look at this little box. I am sure

Sally's Souvenir Shop
St Philips

one of my friends will like it," said Kristy. "St. Philip" was spelled out in colored stones.

"It is great," I said. "I like these mirrors, too."

They were hand-sized mirrors with seashells glued to the back. The shells spelled out "St. Philip." I picked out a heart-shaped one for Hannie.

Sniff, sniff. I followed my nose to a shelf where little bags were hanging from strings. They were about the size of tea bags and smelled like flowers.

"Those are spirit bags. They drive away bad spirits and bring the wearer good luck," said the saleswoman.

I picked one out for Nancy.

On the shelf below was a box of St. Philip's seashell keychains. I bought one for Seth. (He has a lot of keys.)

"Come on, Karen," said Kristy. "It is time to get back to the van."

We each handed the woman some St. Philip's money. (Daddy had traded in our

American money for island money at the hotel.) The saleswoman handed me back a couple of coins.

"Uh-oh," I said.

"What is wrong?" asked Kristy.

"I have spent almost all my money. But I have not found a gift for Daddy. And his birthday is only six days away," I said.

"Do not worry. Instead of buying him a gift, you could do something special for him," said Kristy. "You could make up a song or something and perform it for him."

This sounded like a good idea. I felt relieved. I just hoped it would be a good enough gift for Daddy.

Sandy's Secret

"See you later, everyone!" I called.

It was Tuesday morning. David Michael and I were heading out for our second morning at the Island Club.

When we reached the poolhouse Mark had just finished putting a net across the pool.

"Hi!" I said. "What are we going to play?"

"We are going to try a game of water volleyball," replied Mark.

"Cool," I said.

Just then Sandy arrived. I ran to meet her.

"We are going to play water volleyball in the pool," I said. "Do you want to be on my team?"

"No. I don't feel like playing," replied Sandy.

"Why not? You did not go in the water yesterday. You do not want to miss out two days in a row, do you?" I asked.

"I will see you later," said Sandy. "I am going to tell Jenny I want to do something else instead."

Before I could say another word, Sandy was gone. I saw Jenny setting her up with art supplies at a table. Two other kids who did not feel like going in the water sat with her.

I was sorry Sandy did not want to play. Water volleyball was gigundoly fun. And my team won. Yea!

When we finished, Jenny told us to meet her on the beach to play dodgeball.

I sat next to Sandy for a moment.

"Come on, Sandy," I said. "Let's be teammates."

"I am making a card. I want to finish it," replied Sandy.

"I know you did not want to join the Island Club. But since you are in it, you may as well have some fun," I said.

"I am having fun making the card," replied Sandy.

"Karen! We are waiting for you," called Jenny.

"When we finish playing dodgeball, maybe we will do something you like. Then we could do it together," I said.

"Maybe," replied Sandy.

I ran to the beach to join the others. I got hit with the ball right away. Boo and bullfrogs.

When the game ended, Jenny gathered everyone together for a singalong on the beach. Guess what. Sandy joined us. I sat next to her.

We sang some silly songs. One of my

favorites is "The Baby Bumble Bee." At the end we sang, "Buzzy, buzzy, buzzy. Ooooh, it bit me!" I made believe I was stinging Sandy.

"We have time for one more quick swim," said Jenny.

I turned to Sandy.

"Want to be my buddy?" I asked.

"No, thank you, I do not," she replied.

"Come *on*. Just take *one* swim with me, *please?*"

"I cannot do that, okay? Leave me alone."

"Not until you tell me why you won't go swimming," I replied. "I won't make fun of you or anything. Are you afraid of the water? If you are, I could help you."

Sandy sighed. Then she pulled me aside and said, "I am not afraid of the water. I do not think I should go swimming because I had open-heart surgery last year."

Wow. I did not expect to hear that. I knew that could be serious because my grandad had open-heart surgery. I wanted to say something nice to Sandy so she would not feel so bad.

"You look very healthy," I said. "Do you feel okay?"

"The doctors say I am fine and can do anything I want. But I still think I should take it easy. I do not think swimming would be a good thing for me to do."

I heard Jenny call everyone out of the water. Our parents were arriving to pick us up.

I had missed my swim. But I did not mind. I was glad Sandy had told me her secret. Maybe now we could be friends.

"See you tomorrow," I said.

I saw Daddy waiting and ran to meet him.

A Delicious Day

"Who's hungry?" asked Daddy.

"I am!" I replied.

"Me, too," said David Michael.

"Robert's van is leaving for town at twelve-thirty sharp," said Daddy. "Everyone is upstairs getting ready."

My family was in the rooms changing into clothes to wear to town. Everyone had had a great morning.

At 12:20 we rode the elevators downstairs to meet the van. On the way Sam bragged about his golf game to anyone who would listen.

"I only took a few classes at school, but the game came back to me fast. I am a pretty good golfer," said Sam.

"What about me?" asked Nannie. "I expect to win the grand prize. It is a silver cup and dinner for four at the nicest restaurant on the island."

"Do not forget what Laura said about the other players," said Elizabeth. "Some of them are very good."

"I am not worried about them," said Nannie.

"You may have to worry about beating me," said Sam.

He sounded as though he were joking. But I think he meant it a little bit. I wished Sam and Nannie were not in the same tournament. Who would I root for? I did not want either of them to feel bad if the other person won.

Beep! Beep! The van had pulled up outside the lobby door. We piled in.

"What are you up to this afternoon, my friend?" asked Robert.

"We are going to have lunch in town," I replied.

"I know just the place. Chester's Chicken. Chester is my cousin. He makes the best chicken in town," said Robert.

"You have a lot of cousins don't you?" I said.

"You are not the only one with a big family," replied Robert.

"I bet my family is bigger than yours," I said.

I sat at the front of the van and told Robert about my two families. Then he told me about his family. Guess what. His family was even bigger than mine!

Daddy wrote down the directions to Chester's Chicken.

"Tell him Robert sent you!" called our friend as we climbed out of the van.

The restaurant was small with a beaded curtain for a door. Daddy introduced himself to Chester and told him that Robert had sent us.

"Any friend of my cousin's is a friend of mine. Sit down and make yourselves at home," said Chester.

There were three kinds of chicken to choose from. Each had a funny name. The name told you how spicy the chicken was. There was peace-and-quiet, have-some-fun, and get-out-the-fire-extinguisher.

David Michael, Andrew, Emily, Elizabeth, and I ordered peace-and-quiet.

Daddy and Kristy ordered have-some-fun. (I tasted a piece. I did not think it was fun at all.)

Sam, Charlie, and Nannie ordered get-out-the-fire-extinguisher. Their eyes teared up and their noses ran. They said it was the best chicken they ever ate.

We also ordered drinks, french fries, and coleslaw. When we finished eating, Kristy and I led everyone to the Cheap Stop Food Market.

Daddy told us we had to stick with buddies in the market because it was so big and crowded. That made me think about Sandy. She had seemed very sad and worried. I wished she would let me be her friend. I could cheer her up.

We bought six different kinds of fruit for dessert. Then we went to a park in the center of town to eat it. I ate a piece of mango and two slices of watermelon.

We brought Robert some fruit for his family. He thanked us for the gift. We thanked him for sending us to Chester's Chicken.

It had been a delicious day.

My Island Club Friend

On Wednesday I went to the Island Club with a plan. The plan was not to be pushy with Sandy. When I arrived, she was sitting alone on a bench by the poolhouse.

"Hi, Sandy. Do you want to hear what I did with my family yesterday?" I asked.

I thought that was a very unpushy thing to say.

"No thanks," replied Sandy.

"You could tell me about your afternoon if you want. I will just listen," I said.

"I do not feel like talking now."

The old pushy me would have asked why. The new unpushy me said, "Maybe later you will feel like talking."

"Let's get started, Island Clubbers!" said Jenny. "Who wants to have a water relay race? All in favor say *aye*!"

"Aye!" shouted almost all the Island Clubbers.

I knew Sandy would not want to be in a water relay race. But I did not say one word. I pinched my lips shut and headed down to the water. Being unpushy is hard.

Being in a water relay race is easy. And fun. There were five of us on each team. I was first on line. Jenny handed me a Ping-Pong ball. When she blew her whistle, I was supposed to swim to a red buoy, tap it twice, and swim back to my team. I swam fast. Everyone on my team swam fast. We won by a mile!

After the race, Jenny asked everyone to gather around for a club meeting. Sandy sat down between two girls. I squeezed in next to her. (Oops. That was a little bit pushy.)

"I thought it would be fun for us to play some games with the Dolphin Club tomorrow," said Jenny. "Let's decide together what games we should play."

"My sister Emily likes Simon says. My brother Andrew likes duck, duck, goose," I said.

Jenny made a list of the games we suggested. We voted for three games. We picked Simon says; duck, duck, goose; and let's go fishing.

"I also thought it would be nice to make gifts for the Dolphin Clubbers," said Jenny. "I have some small visors. We can decorate them now and hand them out tomorrow."

I turned to Sandy and asked in a very unpushy way, "Do you want to sit next to me?"

Sandy did not even answer. She stood up and sat at a table by herself. That made me mad. I marched over to the table where she was sitting.

"I am only trying to be your friend," I said.

"Well, I do not *want* another friend!" replied Sandy.

"Why not?"

"When kids find out I have a heart condition they stop wanting to be my friend. It is even worse when I tell them I had surgery," replied Sandy. "So I don't want friends because friends do not last anyway."

"Those kids were being silly. I know plenty of people who have had surgery. Even my best friend, Nancy Dawes. She had her appendix out. We did not stop being friends for one minute. So you do not have to worry about *me*," I said.

Sandy smiled. It was just a little smile. Then she scooted over on the bench. I sat down next to her.

"I have one brother and one sister in the Dolphin Club," I said. "That means I have to make two visors."

"I can make one for you," said Sandy.

"Thanks. You can make the visor for Andrew," I said.

Sandy took a visor and squeezed glue in the shape of an A onto it. Then she sprinkled on green glitter.

"What did you do with your family yesterday?" asked Sandy.

I told her about Chester's Chicken. Sandy told me about the drive she took with her parents. We talked and worked on the visors. I felt good. Finally I had an Island Club friend.

A

Emily the Fish

I ate lunch with my family on the beach. When we finished, Nannie and Sam hurried off to work on their golf games. Daddy and Elizabeth looked for hammocks to read in. Charlie took David Michael, Andrew, and Emily to the beach. And I went for a walk around Palm Isle with Kristy.

"I thought of what I want to do for Daddy's birthday," I told Kristy. "I have decided to write a skit about friendship and perform it."

"That sounds great," replied Kristy.

"I am glad you think so," I said. "Because I would like you to be in my skit."

"Oh, Karen, do I have to? I am not really in the mood to be in a skit. It sounds like work and I am on vacation."

"But you would do the best job because you are my friend," I said. (I had thought about asking Sandy. But we were just starting to be friends. And I would not have enough time to rehearse with her.)

"Okay," replied Kristy. "After all, what are friends for if not to help each other out."

"Thanks!" I said. "Will you help me write it, too?"

"Ka-ren! Whose gift is this anyway? Yours or mine?"

"It is mine," I replied. "But I need a little help from my big sister and good friend."

"Do not push your luck," said Kristy, grinning.

We looked for a shady spot to sit in while we worked on the skit. On the way, we passed the golf course. We did not see Nannie and Sam. But we did see some of the other players.

"They look pretty good," said Kristy. "I hope Nannie and Sam will not be too disappointed if they do not win the tournament."

"I hope so, too," I replied.

We walked until we found a bench under a tree. We sat down and put our heads together. We came up with some good ideas. But after awhile we got stuck.

"Come on," said Kristy. "Let's go to the beach. We can work on the skit later."

We ran to find our brothers and sister. They were building a sand castle by the water. We sat down and helped them. Then we all decided to go in the water. Charlie got water wings for Emily. Then we found a calm, shallow spot.

"Karen and Emily, you can be buddies," said Charlie. "David Michael and Andrew can be buddies. Kristy and I will be watching in case you need us."

I took Emily's hand and walked a few steps with her into the water.

"Whee!" shouted Emily.

She started splashing water. We walked a few more steps. Suddenly Emily dunked down and paddled around like a puppy.

"Look who can swim!" I said.

Emily jumped up and clapped her hands. Then she dunked down again and paddled around some more.

"Hooray for Emily!" we all called.

Round and round she went. Then she jumped up and started clapping for herself.

"Emily is a fish," she said proudly.

She was very excited. She swam around and around like a mermaid.

Friends

I ran all the way to the Island Club on Thursday morning. I wanted to spend as much time as I could with my new friend. Sandy greeted me with a huge smile.

"Hi!" she said. "I can hardly wait till the Dolphin Club gets here. I want to meet Andrew and Emily."

"They want to meet you, too," I replied. I told Sandy how Emily had started to swim yesterday.

"That is great," said Sandy.

"Okay, everyone! We have time for a

quick swim before the Dolphin Club gets here," said Jenny.

"Are you sure you do not want to come?" I asked.

"I am sure," replied Sandy. "I will see you later."

I ran to join the others. I love the Caribbean Sea. It is just the right temperature. And sometimes little schools of fish swim by. They are tiny fish and not one bit scary.

For awhile I floated on my back and looked at the sky. Then some kids started a game of water tag and I joined in. I had just finished my turn at being it when Jenny blew her whistle.

"It is time to get ready for our visitors," she said.

I ran to meet Sandy. She showed me the card she had made. On the outside was a picture of a fish with bubbles that spelled Emily. Inside it said *Congratulashons*. At the bottom Sandy had signed her name.

"Emily will love that. You can read it to

her," I said. (I did not tell Sandy that she spelled congratulations wrong.)

All of a sudden we heard little kids shouting and laughing.

"They are here!" called Jenny.

Andrew and Emily ran to say hello to me. I introduced them to Sandy. Sandy read the card to Emily.

"Fish swim. Emily swim!" said Emily.

We handed out the sun visors we had made. The Dolphin Clubbers loved them.

"We are going to play some games," said Jenny. "The Island Clubbers are going to take turns being the leaders. They will play the games, too. I have some prizes for the winners."

I was the first leader in Simon says. I had to call Emily out right away. (She is still too young for that game.) Andrew concentrated very hard. He was the winner. His prize was a plastic monkey on a string.

We played duck, duck, goose. Then we played let's go fishing. Each of us held a stick with a string and a hook at the end. Jenny had scattered prizes on the ground, and we tried to catch them with the hook.

I liked this game best because it was a quiet game that Sandy could play. (She did not play duck, duck, goose because she did not want to run around the circle.) I also liked it because we got to keep the prizes we caught.

My prize was a seashell in a plastic bottle. Sandy won the same prize. Only the bottle was a different color.

Suddenly, I heard Andrew crying. David Michael and I ran to him to see what was wrong.

"I dropped my monkey in the sand and I cannot find it!" he cried.

We all began to look for it. Andrew just stood there crying. Then Sandy talked to him for a moment and he stopped.

Nobody found the monkey. But Andrew seemed to have forgotten about it. That is because Sandy had given him her shell in the bottle.

"That was really nice of you," I said.

Sandy smiled.

"I will be right back," I said.

I found Jenny and told her what had happened. She gave me another prize to give to Sandy. She did not have another shell in a bottle. But she had a cool whistle shaped like a coconut. I handed it to Sandy.

"Thanks," said Sandy. "That was really nice of *you*."

"That's what friends are for," I replied.

Snorkeling

It was Friday, the last day of the Island Club. That was the bad news. The good news was we were going snorkeling!

"You are going to get to see all kinds of beautiful fish and plants today," said Jenny. "I have masks and snorkels for each of you. We will walk down the beach and find a quiet, shallow area away from the other swimmers. No one has to go in deep water or do anything scary."

I looked at Sandy. Maybe she would try snorkeling.

"You could swim alongside Mark," I whispered.

"I better not," Sandy replied.

"Are you sure? It will be fun."

I could tell Sandy wanted to go. She knew it was not going to be scary or dangerous. But she would not change her mind.

"I do not want to take any chances," said Sandy.

"Well, okay. I will tell you about everything I see," I said.

I was disappointed. But I did not want to push. I did not want to make Sandy feel any worse than she already did.

We walked to a quiet spot on the beach. Sandy spread a towel on the sand and made herself comfortable. Jenny and Mark helped the rest of us put on our masks.

"Let's go," said Jenny. She led us into the water.

"Try to talk quietly and do not move around too much," said Mark. "The quieter we are the more we will see."

I waded in slowly. Then I put my face in the water and looked through my mask. I could not believe the things I was seeing. At school we had read a book called *The Magic School Bus on the Ocean Floor*. I had learned a lot about life underwater. Now I was seeing some of it for real. I saw butterfly fish and angel fish. I saw a school of anchovies. I saw turquoise sea coral and hot pink sponges.

I took a photograph in my mind so I could tell Sandy what I had seen.

I heard Jenny calling and I lifted my head.

"Those of you who are comfortable in deeper water can come out a little farther with me," she said.

I followed her, along with David Michael and a few other kids. We swam under the water with our tubes up in the air so we could breathe. My eyes opened wide when I saw one of my favorite sea creatures swim by. It was a turtle. I love turtles! The turtle seemed to be looking at me. I waved to him. He waved back. (At least I think he waved. He may just have been paddling.)

I wished I could turn into a fish and stay underwater all day. But it was time to go. Jenny was leading us back to shore. I ran to meet Sandy.

"Did you have fun?" she asked.

"It was great. Maybe you will try it another time," I said.

Our parents were at the poolhouse when we returned to the Island Club.

"Do you want to play together later?" asked Sandy.

"Sure. I will ask if it is okay," I said.

Daddy said it was fine with him. He talked with Sandy's parents. They planned for us to meet at the coffee shop after lunch.

It was going to be an exciting afternoon. I would get to play with Sandy. Then we would watch the big golf tournament. Hmm. I wondered who was going to win.

The Big Secret

"Can we go by ourselves?" I asked. "Can we puh-*lease*?"

We had just finished lunch. Sandy and I wanted to go off on our own.

"I don't know if that is a good idea," said Daddy.

"We will be very careful," I said. "We will not go swimming. We will not go far from the hotel. We will wear sunscreen and sun visors and not talk to strangers."

I tried to think of all the things grown-ups worry about.

"We will not even be gone long," said Sandy. "We will be back in time to see the golf tournament."

Finally our parents agreed we could go.

"Yippee!" we shouted.

We held hands and raced to the beach. First we went on a seashell hunt. Then we built a sand castle with some kids from the Island Club. (It looked great until someone's little brother stomped on it.)

"I will be right back," I said to Sandy. "I am going to wash the sand off myself."

When I came back I had an idea.

"You know what?" I said. "If we went out in the ocean just a little way, you probably could see some of the things I saw when I went snorkeling."

"Oh, no. We promised we wouldn't," replied Sandy.

"We promised we would not go *swimming*," I said. "This is not swimming. It is just wading. We will not go far."

"I guess you are right," said Sandy. "I

watched you snorkeling this morning. You were not swimming. At first. It looked like something I really could do."

"Come on, then!" I said.

We headed out into the water. At first it just covered our toes. We went a little farther. It splashed around our ankles. We kept walking till the water was up to our knees.

"We have gone pretty far," said Sandy, looking back.

"So what? It is not deep here," I replied. "And look! There are fish! Do you see them?"

Sandy looked down.

"Wow. They are gorgeous!" she said.

Her smile was about a mile wide.

"And there is sea coral," I said.

We were standing in a great spot. We saw everything I had seen except for the pink sponges and the waving turtle.

I saw something move a little way out. It looked as though it might be the turtle after all.

"Come on," I said.

We waded out a little farther. It turned out it was not the turtle. It was a piece of dark seaweed floating by.

I could see lots of interesting things. But the interesting things seemed to be deeper and deeper under the water. That is because the water was getting higher and higher.

"Uh-oh. I think the tide is coming in. We have to go back," I said. "We have to *swim* to shore!"

"I can't! It is too far!" shouted Sandy.

"You do not have a choice," I said. "You have to swim. Now. Let's go."

The most important thing was to remain calm. If we swam slowly and did not panic, we could make it back.

We swam side by side all the way. Once Sandy swallowed water and started coughing. It was scary. We stopped and treaded water. Then we started again.

Finally the shore seemed closer. I felt my feet brush the sand. Sandy stood up first.

"You did it!" I shouted.

"Hey, I did! I really did!" replied Sandy. She sounded surprised — and gigundoly happy.

We dropped down onto the beach to rest. Then it hit us. We had done a very foolish and dangerous thing. We could have drowned.

"We better not tell anyone," I said.

"Not a soul," replied Sandy.

We had a big secret to keep.

The Golf Tournament

"I will meet you back in the lobby in five minutes," I said. "Unless one of us gets caught!"

We sneaked upstairs to our rooms to change into dry clothes. Luckily no one was there. Everyone was probably already at the golf course. The tournament was about to begin.

"Let's hurry," I said when we met in the lobby. "If we are late, they might ask us questions."

We ran most of the way. When we were

almost there, we stopped and walked. We did not want to look out of breath.

Sandy's parents and my family were standing together.

"Did you two have a good time?" asked Sandy's mother.

Sandy just nodded.

"Look! There are Nannie and Sam," I said.

They waved to us. We waved back.

"Good luck!" I called. I was not sure which of them I was wishing good luck. If one of them won, the other might feel bad. Maybe it would be better if neither of them won the tournament, I thought. But I knew they both wanted to win badly.

During the last few days, golf was practically all either of them talked about. They even took turns standing around swinging make-believe golf clubs.

"Here we go," said Daddy. "It is Nannie's turn. Everyone be quiet so she can concentrate."

Click! Nannie's golf club hit the ball. The

ball sailed up in the air. It dropped down on a dark patch of grass and rolled toward a hole in the ground.

"Yea, Nannie!" I shouted.

Oops. I was the only one making noise. Everyone else was clapping quietly. I guess golf is a quiet kind of game. Sandy and I giggled because I had made so much noise.

Two other people took their turns. Their balls did not get as close to the hole as Nannie's.

Then it was Sam's turn. His ball drifted off to the side.

The middle of the game was kind of boring. Sandy and I sat down on the grass and looked for interesting bugs. Things started getting exciting again at the end of the game.

I heard one woman say she was surprised there were so many good players in the tournament. A man said Nannie was one of the best. Sam did not seem to mind that Nannie was doing better than he was. He kept patting her on the back. He looked very proud.

Now I could root for Nannie without feeling bad about Sam. Each time someone took a turn, the clapping grew louder. People were starting to whisper about who they thought would win. Guess what. It was Nannie. Nannie won the tournament.

Ron, the hospitality director, shook Nannie's hand and gave her a silver cup and an envelope with dinner tickets in it.

"Congratulations," he said. "Are you surprised you won?"

"Not really," replied Nannie. "I am just very happy."

We all hugged Nannie.

"We are so proud of you," said Elizabeth.

"You played a great game," said Sam.

"Tomorrow night I want to take *everybody* to dinner at Dominique's Restaurant. It will be my treat," said Nannie.

She even invited Sandy and her parents to come as her guests. This was great. It would be two parties in one. It would be

NNER
VOUCHER

a tournament party for Nannie and a birthday party for Daddy.

I had already written a very good friendship skit and rehearsed it with Kristy. After a couple more rehearsals, I was sure we would be ready.

Party Plans

The minute I woke up on Saturday morning, I started thinking about Daddy's party.

Kristy had already taken Emily downstairs to have breakfast. I was looking in the closet trying to decide what I would wear to our party when Elizabeth came into the room.

"What should I wear to dinner tonight?" I asked. "I want to look extra nice for Daddy's birthday party."

"Birthday party?" said Elizabeth. "Oh, my goodness! I forgot all about your father's birthday. I think everyone has. Even your father."

"Kristy and I did not forget. We have been rehearsing a birthday skit I wrote for him," I said proudly. "And I thought Nannie was taking us all for a birthday dinner."

"We will just have to turn it into a birthday dinner," replied Elizabeth. "Thank you for remembering, Karen."

Suddenly there were a million things to do. I helped Elizabeth make a list. I felt gigundoly important being the birthday party organizer.

"Let's try to keep this a secret from Daddy. Since he has forgotten his birthday, we will make it a surprise party for him," said Elizabeth.

Just then we heard a knock on the door.

"Are you two coming to breakfast?" asked Daddy.

"In a minute," I replied. "I need Elizabeth to help me with something."

"See you downstairs," said Daddy.

"Here is the plan," said Elizabeth. "I will

go into town with Nannie, Kristy, and Emily to buy some gifts. We will stop at Dominique's Restaurant and see if they can make a cake for us. Do you think you and Sandy could make some party decorations?"

"Sure we can!" I replied. (I am a very good decoration maker.)

It was a hectic day. Sam and Charlie asked Daddy to go sailing with them. Right after breakfast, Elizabeth, Nannie, Kristy, and Emily boarded Robert's van heading for town.

"Um, Kristy, I have a question," I said before they left. "You will not be able to rehearse with me today because you are going to town. And Sandy is coming to the dinner. So I was thinking maybe she could be in the skit with me instead of you."

I was afraid I was going to hurt Kristy's feelings. But I did not have anything to worry about. She looked very relieved.

"That is a terrific idea," said Kristy. "I am sure you two will do a great job."

I waved good-bye, then went off to find Sandy. She loved the idea of being in the skit with me.

"Let's get started," I said. "We have decorations to make and a skit to rehearse. We have a lot of work to do."

Happy Birthday, Daddy

"Ah, yes. The party of thirteen," said Dominique's headwaiter with a smile. "Right this way, please."

He led us to our table. Sandy and I were each wearing brand-new party dresses. That afternoon, we had met a woman on the beach who was selling clothes. Our dresses were handmade and tie-dyed. All the colors we saw at the fruit market were in mine. It was pink, orange, yellow, and green. Sandy's dress was different shades of blue. It looked like the sea and the sky.

"You girls look beautiful for Nannie's celebration," said Daddy.

"Thank you," we replied.

I squeezed Sandy's hand. Daddy still did not know the party was for him. We had done a good job of keeping the surprise. Robert had helped. He had hidden Daddy's gifts on the van and dropped them off at the restaurant when he finished work. (We invited him to the party. But he wanted to go home to his family.)

I watched Daddy's face as we walked into our private room at the back of the restaurant and shouted, "Surprise! Happy birthday!"

Daddy was so happy. He was beaming.

The room looked gigundoly great. Balloons and streamers were everywhere. There were party hats and horns. Presents were piled high on a table.

"I forgot all about my birthday," he said.

"You can thank Karen for reminding us," said Elizabeth.

"Thank you, sweetheart," said Daddy, giving me a hug.

"You are welcome," I replied. "Daddy, I would like to give you my gift right away. Otherwise I will be too nervous to eat supper."

Putting on a show, even for my family, made me nervous. I had butterflies in my stomach.

"What kind of gift would make you nervous?" asked Daddy.

"You will see," I replied. "Sam, drum-roll, please."

Everyone took a seat. Sam drummed his hands on the table like a real drummer in a band. I grabbed the bag with our costumes. Sandy and I ducked out of the room and put them on. We each wore a mask with whiskers and a cat's tail. We ran back into the room and I introduced the play.

"Sandy and I will be performing together," I said. "The show is called 'Cool Cat Friends.' "

Everyone enjoyed our skit. When we

were done, we read a poem I wrote.

"Someone I know likes you well and true.

"If she were not a scaredy cat, she would tell you who."

We went around the room together telling each person why we liked them. When we got to Daddy, I recited a poem all by myself.

"I am the one who likes you well and true.

"Now that it's your birthday I will sing a song to you."

I sang "Happy Birthday," and everyone joined in.

"Bravo!" said Daddy. "Thank you for the wonderful gift."

Everyone clapped for us. I felt gigundoly proud.

We ate a delicious dinner. Then the waiters brought out a pineapple cake with birthday candles. (Pineapple was all they could make on short notice.)

Daddy opened his gifts. He got a lot of St. Philip souvenirs. (I was glad my gift to

Daddy was the skit I wrote. It turned out to be special after all.) Nannie showed off her silver cup. Then we *all* had a surprise.

A band walked into the room playing "Happy Birthday." When they finished, the leader said, "My name is Peter. I am a cousin of Robert's. He sent me as a birthday gift, a tournament gift, and a farewell gift to his favorite family."

Another cousin. I could hardly believe it. Even though Robert could not be at the party, he helped us celebrate our last night on the island. We had a blast!

Pen Pals

The next morning, we were up early getting ready for our flight. I was gigundoly sad to be leaving.

"Karen, did you leave any shells on the island?" asked Kristy.

I laughed. I was taking home an awfully big bunch.

"I think there are a few left on the beach," I replied.

Our flight was scheduled to leave late in the morning. It was a good thing because we had a few small disasters. Andrew lost one of his sneakers. Emily was crying because she was tired. And the lock on Daddy's suitcase got jammed.

But we had solved all our problems by the time we went downstairs for breakfast. We met Sandy and her parents in the coffee shop. They were going home a few hours later than we were. So Sandy and I had plenty of time to say good-bye.

Our parents said it was okay for us to take a walk to the beach when we finished eating. (I was sure we would not get into any trouble. There was not enough time!)

"I wish we lived closer together, so we could visit each other," said Sandy.

"So do I. But we can write to each other. We can be pen pals," I replied.

"I promise to write as soon as I get home," said Sandy.

"I will write to you from the airplane," I said.

"I will write to you before I leave the island!" replied Sandy.

I looked over my shoulder to make sure no one was close enough to hear me.

"We should not have gone so far out in the water yesterday," I whispered. "But you really are a very good swimmer. You should try snorkeling some time."

"I know I am a good swimmer," replied Sandy. "And the doctors and my parents said I can swim and do anything I want. I have just been afraid."

"Well, I think it is time to be brave," I said.

"Karen! We have to go," called Daddy.

Sandy and I ran back to the hotel to exchange addresses. Then we hugged and waved good-bye. The next thing I knew, my family and I were in Robert's van on our way to the airport.

"Thank you for everything," I said to Robert. "Say good-bye to all your cousins for me."

"I will. I hope you will come back to this island very, very soon," replied Robert.

I slept during most of the plane flights.

So I did not get to write to Sandy. I promised myself I would write to her as soon as I got home.

But I was very busy and I forgot. A few days passed. Then a couple of weeks. Then a couple of months. I kept meaning to write. But I never got around to it. I did not receive a letter from Sandy either. She must have been busy, too.

That's the way it is sometimes with pen pals. Then all of a sudden you have a surprise. My first letter from Sandy arrived on a Tuesday, three months after I had returned to Stoneybrook. Here is what it said:

Dear Karen,

Hi! How are you? Sorry it's taken me so long to write. I have been very busy. I have even been swimming!

I have good news. My parents promised that next year we will go back to Palm Isle for spring vacation. Can you come too? I want to go snorkeling. We can go together!

Write back soon.

Love,
Sandy

This was a very good letter. I was happy that Sandy was feeling braver. And I was happy that she knew I was still her friend even though I had forgotten to write.

I did not want to forget again. I took out a piece of pink paper and a purple pen. At the top, I wrote *Dear Sandy*. Then I wrote a long letter. I had a lot I to tell my very good island friend.

About the Author

Ann M. Martin lives in New York City and loves animals, especially cats. She has two cats of her own, Gussie and Woody.

Other books by Ann M. Martin that you might enjoy are *Stage Fright; Me and Katie (the Pest)*; and the books in *The Baby-sitters Club* series.

Ann likes ice cream and *I Love Lucy*. And she has her own little sister, whose name is Jane.

Don't miss #72

KAREN'S NEW PUPPY

I knew we were supposed to be going cage by cage. But a puppy at the end of the row was looking right at me. Her tail was wagging. I could hear it thump, thump, thumping on the cage floor. I could not wait. I ran to meet her.

She had golden fur and big brown eyes. She poked her nose through the bars of the cage and licked my face.

"Andrew, come look!" I called.

Andrew raced over. He reached out to pet the puppy. She licked his hand.

"I like her. Can she be our puppy?" he said.

Mommy and Seth came to see her.

"She is sweet and frisky," said Mommy.

"I will ask Joe if he can take her out," said Seth.

Guess who got to hold the puppy first.

Amber Brown has *big* plans for her vacation!

Amber's off to visit her aunt in London, and she's one excited kid before she gets there. But she's one *itchy* kid when she arrives. Mosquito bites, she thinks. Chicken pox, she finds out.

YOU CAN'T EAT YOUR CHICKEN POX, AMBER BROWN

by Paula Danziger

Coming this March to bookstores everywhere.

And don't miss Amber's other adventure:
AMBER BROWN IS NOT A CRAYON

SCHOLASTIC